MAXi
AND THE
THREE BERRIES

WRITTEN BY BILL KROYER

ILLUSTRATED BY TODD DAKINS

One of Four Stories
in The Adventures of Taxi Dog Series

see-saw

publishing

Text by Bill Kroyer • Illustrations by Todd Dakins

Book design by Noble Pursuits LLC with art direction by Elaine Noble

Copyright © 2017 by Taxi Dog Productions LLC
Adapted from the script by Bill Kroyer
Based upon the original book *The Adventures of Taxi Dog* written by and with
original characters by Sal & Debra Barracca and originally illustrated by Mark Buehner

www.maxiandthethreeberries.com • www.peekaboopublishing.com

See-Saw Publishing
Part of the Peek-A-Boo Publishing Group

FIrst Edition 2017 • Printed by Shenzhen TianHong Printing Co., Ltd. in Shenzhen, China

ISBN: 978-1-943154-93-7 (Hardback)
ISBN: 978-1-943154-92-0 (Paperback)

10 9 8 7 6 5 4 3 2 1

PEEK - A - BOO

PUBLISHING GROUP

Maxi sits alone in the Taxi waiting for Jim
outside the Donut Hub Bakery in New York City.

Jim opens the driver's door holding a paper sack.
"Look what I've got for us," says Jim. "Take a whiff, Maxi."

Maxi's whiskers tickle when dipping into the sack.
"Woof," gurgles Maxi.

Jim reaches into the sack and lifts out two fluffy donut holes. "And you know the best part?"

Maxi's head shakes an emphatic 'No!'.

"They taste even better than they smell!"

"Should we wait to eat these after lunch? I don't know if I can resist."

Maxi's head shakes 'no' again.

Just then, a man climbs into the back seat of the taxi.
"Twenty-five East Fifty-first Street, please!"

A disappointed Maxi watches as Jim drops the donut holes back into the sack.

"Yes, sir," says Jim. "We'll have you there faster than you can say honey-glazed maple logs."

"Is your dog friendly?" asks the man.

"Say hello to the man, Maxi," says Jim.

Maxi pops up and holds out a paw for the man to shake.

"Rruff!"

"Nice to meet you, Maxi. I'm Danny Devine of Divine Delectables."

Danny is holding a large white bakery box. He opens the box for Maxi to see. Jim looks back in the rear view mirror. It's an edible bouquet. All fresh fruit--bananas, pineapple, strawberries--sculpted into a fairy tale creation. I call it the Three Berries. Get it?"

Danny has turned the box
around so the open lid blocks
the fruit from Maxi's view.

Jim wheels the taxi into a spot in front
of an East Side brownstone.

"Here we are. Twenty-five East Fifty-first.
That'll be…"

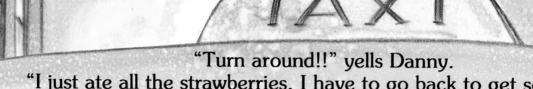

"Turn around!!" yells Danny.
"I just ate all the strawberries. I have to go back to get some more before I deliver this bouquet or my business will be ruined."

"Why did you do that?" asks Jim.

"I don't know. I do it all the time.
I can't resist eating the strawberries."

Jim races back to Danny's shop.

"There's no place to park," yells Jim.
"Maxi can go in to the shop to help you redo your creation."

"Just look at these beauties.
I'm tempted to eat every one of them,"
says Danny.

Maxi stares at a big pastrami
sandwich on the table.

"There are only twelve strawberries left. I need three strawberries for each of the three berry 'sculptures'. How many strawberries will be left over?" asks Danny.

"Arf, arf, arf."

Maxi has one eye glued onto the pastrami sandwich and one eye glued to Danny and the strawberries.

Danny reaches out for a berry to sneak into his mouth.
But Maxi sees him and moans, "Hmmm."

While Maxi is staring at the sandwich, Danny pops the strawberry into his mouth.

Maxi turns around to see Danny eating the strawberry and moans louder.

Danny pops another strawberry into his mouth.

"I just can't resist these big red juicy berries," slurps Danny.

Maxi licks his lips while looking at the sandwich.

But, Maxi is resisting the urge to devour the sandwich.

Danny turns to take another
strawberry and Maxi gets
right into his face.

"Hmmm," moans Maxi
as loudly as possible.

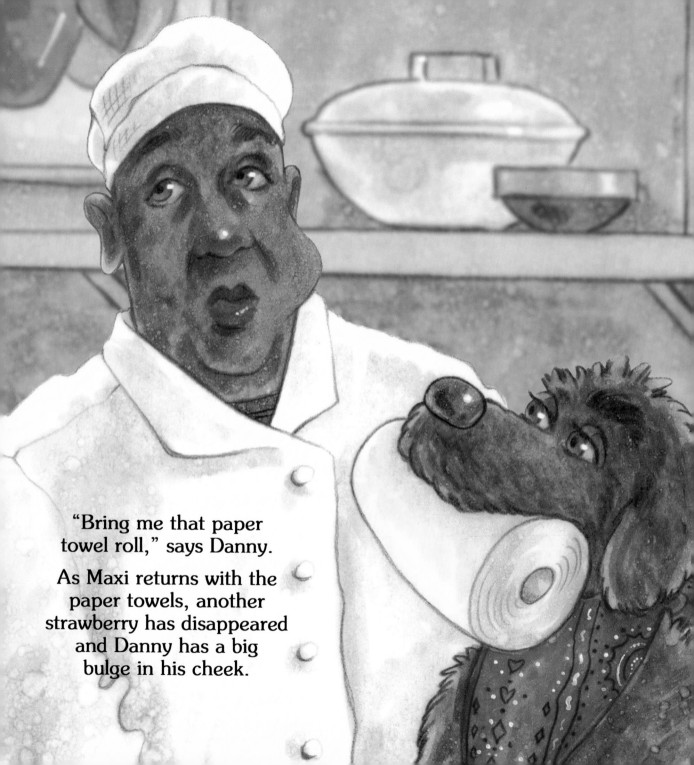

"Bring me that paper towel roll," says Danny.

As Maxi returns with the paper towels, another strawberry has disappeared and Danny has a big bulge in his cheek.

Danny replaces the berries on the papa bear and the mama bear. He puts two strawberries on the baby bear for eyes. Just one strawberry left for the nose.

Danny lifts the last strawberry up to his lips. "This is the best one of all..."

Maxi gently puts his paws on Danny's hand and pushes it down.

"Arrr," Maxi whines.

"If you let me eat this berry, I'll let you eat the pastrami sandwich."

"Maxi looks at the sandwich then closes his eyes and takes a deep breath."

Danny follows Maxi's example, takes a deep breath and remembers his goal of finishing his creation."

Danny puts the last strawberry in place.

"There, see, they are all done," says Danny.
"The Three Berries."

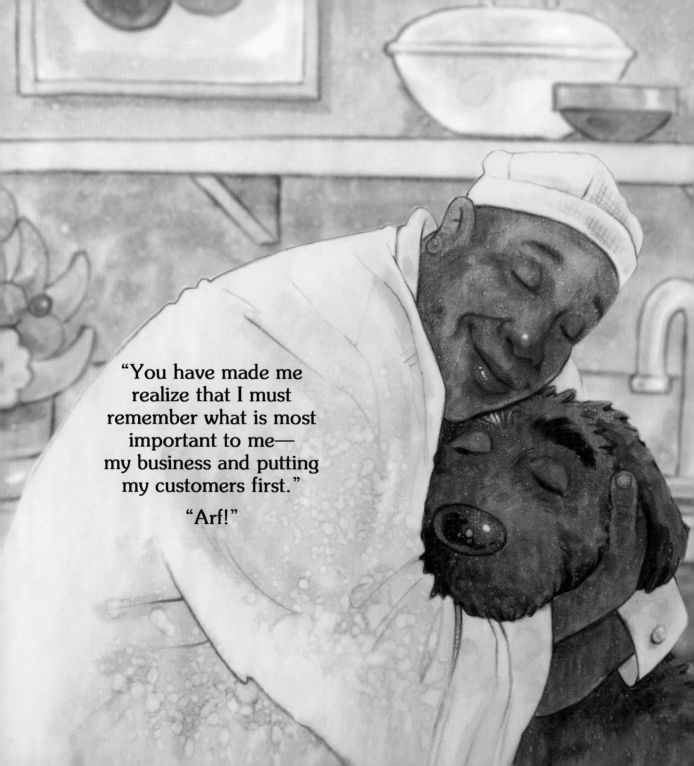

"You have made me realize that I must remember what is most important to me— my business and putting my customers first."

"Arf!"

"Now, you have earned that sandwich
you have had your eyes on."

"Woof! Woof!"

Danny and Maxi come back out of the shop to the taxi.
Danny holds up a bag.

"Everything go all right in there?" asks Jim.

"Maxi was a great helper," says Danny with a wink.
"There is a pastrami sandwich for both of you in this bag."

Jim and Maxi drive Danny to Twenty-five East Fifty-first Street.
They wave as they drop off Danny to deliver his sculpture.

"It was nice of Danny to give us this
pastrami sandwich wasn't it, Maxi?"

"Woof!"

"Let's stop at the park for lunch.
And then we can finally have those donut holes for dessert!"

"Rruff!"

The End